MW00885378

and Julian

All rights reserved, no part of this publication
may be reproduced

copyright 2021 Nancy Montgomery

ISBN 978-1-7374052-1-4

Khaekave Arts

GOOD MORNING

ENCINITAS

written and illustrated by
Nancy Montgomery

Our window's wide open
birds singing their songs

Wake up, Encinitas
a new day has dawned

Good morning, Birds!

They start in the morning and go 'till twilight
it's dogs walking owners that make such a sight

Strolling down Neptune, with leashes or not
our dogs are so happy to be out for a trot

Poodles and doodles, shepherds and hounds
so many kinds, you'll hear all their sounds

Come say hello and they'll happily talk
these neighborhood dogs, out for a walk

Down on the highway, the baker's been working
he's filled up his cases to sweeten our morning

Donuts with sprinkles, crullers with glaze
whatever your taste, he's sure to amaze

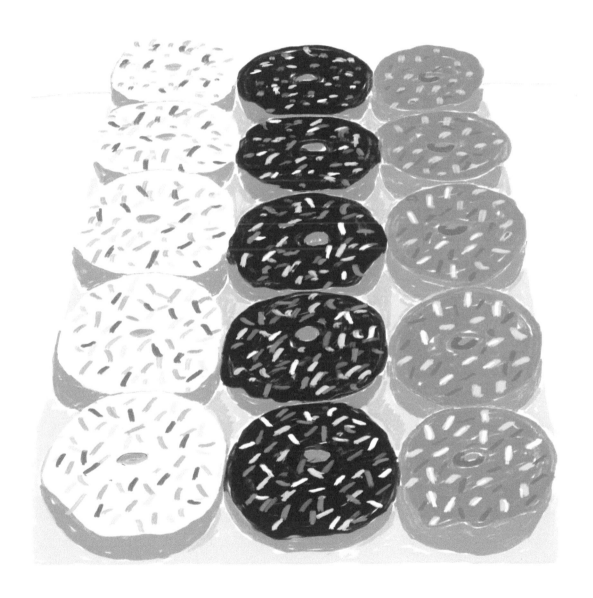

Hello ficus trees, so tall and grand
all around town like sentries you stand

Under your branches there's shade for us all
and above for the birds, a home ever so tall

Down the steps in the morning dawn
the swimmers get going with nary a yawn

Out through the waves, they turn toward Moonlight
then swim straight ahead, the buoy in sight

With pelicans above and fish below
it's a round trip for them, in the ocean they know

With fold-out chairs
and umbrellas in hand

We play on the beach
our toes in the sand

Bring buckets and shovels
there are castles to make

Searching for shells
we'll find treasures to take

With the sun in our faces
and wind in our hair

Let's dive through the waves
breathing salt air

As Summer winds down
there's a contest in town

At the base of the steps, and out in the sand
the surfers line up, by their longboards they stand

With the waves big and glassy, and the incoming tide
our friends all head out, grabbing waves for the ride

At the end of the morning, when the last heat is done
we'll wait for the party to find out who's won

It's time for lunch
let's see what's cooking

With Juanita's right there
no need for more looking

At our favorite taco shop
it's never too late

For burritos, tostadas
and a taco plate

From the first step inside
it's "hello, amigo!"

Just pick from the menu
for here or to go

Racers and cruisers, e-bikes and trikes
cycling is something everyone likes
With bikes whizzing by, some fast, some slow
let's hop on our bikes, we've got places to go

Once by the tracks in the middle of town
there was even a flag to wave the trains down

Then they picked up the station and towed it up main street
now it sits by the highway serving good things to eat

It's the Pannikin, you see, so let's go for a break
we can sit for awhile or find something to take

On the edge of town
at the top of the cliff

With glittering dome
and arches aglow

A temple beckons
to the surf break below

Indoors and out
studio and beach

So many places
to learn what they teach

Keep stretching and flexing
practice a pose

It's a way to feel calm
right down to your toes

Keno's on the highway
is always open late

It's a place for home cooking
where you know the price is great

For dessert there's gelato, and a spot just nearby
let's walk down main street and give it a try

Turn in the gate, what else can we do
there's chocolate and lemon, pistachio too

Each day with new flavors, it's so hard to choose
you can taste a few samples, there's nothing to lose

In a cup or a cone, I'll have mine with a spoon
better get going, there's a movie on soon

At the top of the rise a theater awaits
a place we all know, for nights out on dates

It's La Paloma, a landmark they say
with classic marquee saying what's on for today

No Cineplex, multiplex, and no mall in sight
just rows of good seats and a show for tonight

We've washed the salt out of our hair
and the sand between our toes

Our foreheads have been kissed
and our eyes begin to close

Goodnight to our little house
and the breeze that smells of rose

Night-night, birds!

Good-night, Encinitas